KNOCK DOWN GINGER

A.D. Hewitt

This edition first published in paperback by
Michael Terence Publishing in 2022
www.mtp.agency

Copyright © 2022 A.D. Hewitt

A.D. Hewitt has asserted the right to be identified as
the author of this work in accordance with the
Copyright, Designs and Patents Act 1988

ISBN 9781800944213

No part of this publication may be reproduced, stored
in a retrieval system, or transmitted, in any form or
by any means, electronic, mechanical, photocopying,
recording or otherwise, without the prior
permission of the publisher

Cover image
Copyright © Hunter Bliss
www.123rf.com

Cover design
Copyright © 2022 Michael Terence Publishing

Contents

Synopsis 1
Chapter 1: The Scared Girl 3
Chapter 2: The Visit 9
Chapter 3: The Last Hour 13
Chapter 4: The Lost Memories 17
Chapter 5: Emily's Memories of Grandfather 18
Chapter 6: The Masquerade Invitation (The Last Invite) 21
Chapter 7: Strangers and Masqueraders Leave the Masquerade . 24
Chapter 8: Emily's Reflection on the Girl 27
Chapter 9: A Deeper Understanding of Ginger 31
Chapter 10: The Picnic 33
Chapter 11: The Letters 37
Chapter 12: The Accusation 39
Chapter 13: The Stolen Jewels 43
Chapter 14: Emily Alone with Ginger 48
Chapter 15: Girl Friday 52
Chapter 16: The Burglary 55
Chapter 17: Mrs Grant's Deep Concerns 57
Chapter 18: The Watchful Neighbours 60
Chapter 19: The Chance Meeting 62
Chapter 20: Ginger Almost Makes a Confession 66
Chapter 21: The Crime in Society 68
Chapter 22: Ginger's Conversion 70
Epilogue 71

Synopsis

At the ball, Emily met a troubled girl in the drawing room at a manor house.

Ginger was a strange and mysterious country girl.

Emily became friends with Ginger.

During the years, there were burglaries and unsolved crimes. Emily knew Ginger's obsession with jewels. She was obsessed with jewellery! Emily suspected Ginger had an accomplice. Ginger had an obsessional passion for jewels. It was an obsession of hers.

Emily and her mother became vigilant due to Mrs Bridges' house being burgled. Her friend Lorraine lost all of her jewels in a burglary.

Feeling dear love, Emily gave her friend Lorraine her ring, due to her close friend being burgled.

Emily and her mother joined a neighbourhood watch group.

In the meantime, Ginger became reformed and regenerative, due to her guilt and her conscience, Ginger became a Christian. Ginger had a devotion to God.

Ginger taught the children at Sunday School, as well as being a helper when it came to serving refreshments to all of the children there. Emily assisted the children on a few Sundays and attended to those mothers at the crèche, with an obligation as a helper to the children attending Sunday School every Sunday.

Chapter 1:

The Scared Girl

Miss Grant got out of the stagecoach which reached the grand manor house. There the guests came to the ball. She knew some of the guests already. She had been acquainted with them. All of the other strangers she had not known. They were personal friends of Mr and Mrs Burrows.

During the night, Mr Burrows neglected Emily. Mr and Mrs Burrows were occupied with attending to other guests. These people sought their attention with regard to Emily. Mr and Mrs Burrows had been neglectful and negligent to both Emily and his sons.

Emily during the day had been prayerful. Her Christian faith made her strong against adversaries. It protected and defended her against people's wickedness.

The Englishmen and gentlemen desired the attractive woman. Her attractiveness attracted attention. She spoke to acquaintances, the foursome a gardener, painter, art collector and sculptor. Emily showed an enthusiastic interest in them regarding their professions.

"How is the gardening coming on? And your collection of paintings and your still life? And how is the sculpting?"

They all answered at once in acknowledgement.

"Come. Let us show you."

Emily agreed to be shown around. She followed them. Going out of the room, she walked to the hallway. There the dilettante looked at the paintings. The painter took notice of all the reproductions. The painter took them to a room where he had painted a female nude, on a canvas on an easel.

"It's good," remarked Emily.

"I would like to paint you," said the painter.

"Perhaps you can one day," agreed Emily.

Going into another room, Emily admired the sculptures on display and in glass cases.

For a short time, they went outside in the gardens. They admired the lovely gardens and grounds. The gardener was proud of his work. He did horticulture and gardening.

Everywhere groups of guests walked around the manor house, in the grounds and gardens. Mr and Mrs Burrows were popular hosts.

The music could be heard. Dancing took place in the ballroom. Tonight was a romantic moonlit night. The ambience was ideal for a romance, to engage in the pleasure of a romantic encounter.

Most of the guests invited were married couples.

Emily was escorted to the ballroom. There waltzers danced in the ballroom. Emily agreed to dance. She danced with her partner who had offered to dance with her. They joined in the dance, dancing to a waltz, a schmaltz. The waltzers danced. Emily enjoyed the pleasure of a waltz dance. Emily was having an enjoyable time. Emily danced well. Everybody else was having a good time. The waltzers were enjoying their dance, the pleasure of it. Those that did not dance stood and watched the pairs of waltzers dancing. They had a wonderful time dancing.

As the dance ended, Mr and Mrs Burrows came up to Miss Grant. Miss Grant stepped aside as guests moved past in a straight direction, getting out of their way.

"You've come. I didn't think you would come. You're here at last," smiled Mrs Burrows.

"I did say I would come. I have kept my word," said Emily loudly.

"How is work as a beautician?" asked Mr Burrows.

"I have been very busy. It's too much work!" replied Emily.

Mrs Burrows looked at Emily's face and her applied make-up. Emily's stunning attractiveness was quite admirable. A desirable and irresistible Englishwoman.

"Do you have any good beauty tips you can tell me?" asked Mrs Burrows.

"To learn how to apply make-up and to use quality make-up brands," advised Emily.

At this present time, everybody else wanted Mr and Mrs Burrows' attention. With attentiveness, the hosts attended to them.

Feeling exhausted, Emily walked out of the ballroom. She walked through the hallway and then came to the sitting room. At that time, Emily saw a girl crying there. The girl was desperately unhappy and afraid.

"What is wrong?" asked Emily.

The sobbing girl blubbered, "My father has left me. I am alone."

"What are you afraid of? Where is your mother?"

"I am scared of the dark. My mother is dancing," sobbed the girl.

"You are scared of the dark? Well, that makes two of us. When I was a child, I was scared of the dark. I used to scream. I had to sleep with the night light on!" remembered Emily.

The girl was empathic with the stranger's phobia. The sulking girl became less afraid and tense.

"How did you overcome it?"

"I say my prayers at night. I got in the habit of reading the word every day," answered Emily.

All alone, they both came out of the sitting room. Emily led the girl to the ballroom. Emily found the girl's mother, together with her friend.

Emily was agitated at her.

"Your daughter is alone. You shouldn't neglect her."

Emily wondered if the girl's parents were unconcerned.

Emily was uninterested in dancing. She declined the offer to dance. Emily was concerned for the disturbed girl. Emily was in a serious mood. To her surprise, the girl and her parents both decided to leave the ball then. The girl obeyed her mother. The girl was obliged and her mother thankful. In appreciation, they both thanked Emily. With love, the girl shed a tear, and then her tears ran down. Emily embraced the sweet girl.

"Now, say your prayers. Don't forget to say your prayers," urged Emily.

"Oh, I won't forget. Thanks," said the girl sweetly.

Emily waved goodbye and watched them both go. She lost interest in staying at the ball. She took her chance to leave the ball immediately. She hurried out of the manor house, refusing to give any explanation for her departure.

Quickly, Emily got into a stagecoach. Already seated in there was Mrs Dright, a widow, an elderly passenger dressed in black and wearing a shawl.

As soon as the stagecoach reached the main road, Mrs Dright spoke, her voice muffled.

"Who is the girl?" asked Mrs Dright.

"She's someone I met. She's a nice girl. I liked her. She's mysterious," said Emily fondly.

Emily was too upset and saddened. She spoke no more about the uneasy girl, as she felt uneasy talking about it.

On the journey home, Emily nodded off. Emily was relieved to have gone right away.

Chapter 2:

The Visit

Miss Grant visited Mrs Dright at her mansion. Mrs Dright's possessions were a compulsion. Mrs Dright collected antiques. Her husband was an antiques dealer.

Emily admired the furniture and antiques. Everything remained in good condition for all these years. Every fine antique was dusted and polished. In the exact spot. Mrs Dright's antique collection was an obsession. Her obsessiveness with possessions materialistic. Usually, at night, Mrs Dright engaged in a séance with her witch-like friends, as well as hags.

Mrs Dright made the tea. From a tray, Emily took a teacup and saucer and drank it. Mrs Dright sipped her tea and nibbled a biscuit.

"Tell me, child, what was her name?"

"I dunno her name. I didn't ask her," replied Emily.

"She's a dark horse," remarked Mrs Dright.

Emily thought of the mysterious girl as enigmatic.

"She's strange. The boys kept away from the weirdo."

"She hated the boys. She didn't even like one of them."

"Toffee-nose is back," chuckled Emily.

Mrs Dright laughed at Emily's humour.

"This girl is a handful."

Emily recalled the situation.

"When she saw me, she stopped crying. When she had gone, she was relieved. There was no more pain. No more anguish. The girl felt solace. She was glad to get away from those stuck-up boys."

"My dear, my daughter is coming," murmured Mrs Dright.

"Do you want me to go?"

"Yes, you must," paused Mrs Dright. "I am entertaining."

"I will go," mumbled Emily.

"Who was the girl at the ball?"

"I don't know her name. She was a lovely girl. She's disturbed! I kind of felt sorry for her. I had to intervene. The sad thing is, I will never see her again. I do hope I shall see her again."

"That night, I didn't see you much at the ball. Where were you?" said Mrs Dright concernedly.

"I remember I did come to the ball late. I missed most of it. I was far too concerned about the disturbed girl. She was in such a state. I just had to do something for her. It's awful. Her mother neglected her. The girl was sad. I showed my feelings to her, my love and affection. I helped her through the most difficult time in her life. She respected me for it. She appreciated it."

"She did need help."

Emily looked at an old black and white, framed photograph of Mrs Dright.

"I will get going. Thank you for inviting me," thanked Emily.

"That's alright. Do come again, child. Say your prayers."

In agreement, Emily acknowledged Mrs Dright and her profound spirituality.

"Yes, I shall come."

Emily left the mansion at once. She came out of the front door and walked towards the stagecoach. She got into the stagecoach, which took her home.

She respected the hypochondriac and eccentric widow. Emily would visit Mrs Dright again next week.

As soon as Emily got home, Mrs Grant talked about Mrs Dright. Mrs Grant often wondered about the widow dressed in black in mourning.

"How is Mrs Dright?" asked Mother.

"Mrs Dright is fine. She's a cheerful soul! Mrs Dright is down at times. Mrs Dright likes to see me. She makes my tea. We have good conversations. Mrs Dright talks a lot about her late husband. Mrs Dright can't get over the loss of her beloved husband," answered Emily.

"It is understandable. Who can recover from the loss of their loved one? I don't think anyone can."

"Mrs Dright enjoys my company. Mrs Dright loves to have her tea. She likes to talk," smiled Daughter.

"Mrs Dright is an old bitter woman!"

"You don't see eye to eye?" said Daughter.

"We don't. Mrs Dright is fond of you!" replied Mother.

"Mrs Dright does like me. I like to visit Mrs Dright. We get on well together."

"Why does Mrs Dright hurry you up?"

"I guess Mrs Dright wants to see her daughter," said Daughter.

"It's an excuse for her to tell you to go."

"Should I take offence? No… Mrs Dright is a nice woman."

Both daughter and mother stayed together in the living room. They both shared their conversational experiences at High Mount.

Chapter 3:

The Last Hour

Mrs Dright's grandchildren played in the garden. One of them stood by the stumps all ready to bat. Tommy bowled, aiming the tennis ball straight at the stumps. Standing in a batting position, Stan hit a tennis ball hard.

Emily and Mrs Dright watched them playing cricket.

"Watch it! Mind you don't break a window!" warned Mrs Dright.

"We won't. I assure you," said Grandson assuredly.

Mrs Dright grimaced.

"You'd better not!" muttered Mrs Dright.

"Emily, would you like to bat?" asked Stan.

"Me? No! … On second thoughts, I will have a go."

Stan moved out of the way, allowing Emily to stand by the stumps. He got in position to field. He wondered where in anticipation. Emily, batting, stood in front of the stumps. She readily got in position to bat. With a cricket bat, she managed to hit the tennis ball. Stan ran and got the tennis ball. He retrieved it.

"Run!" shouted Mrs Dright.

Emily ran to the other stump without being run out. She walked back to the other stump with the confidence of having no pressure to endure.

Tommy ran and bowled again to Emily. This time Tommy bowled Emily out. The stumps got hit by the bowled tennis ball. In triumph, Tommy raised his arms in the air. He was triumphant at having bowled Emily out.

Emily was humiliated and embarrassed at her batting. She dropped the cricket bat down on the lawn. She'd had enough of playing this game. Her batting was an embarrassment.

She quickly walked away with Mrs Dright. The gentle breeze was light. Going back indoors together, in the drawing room, Emily played draughts with Elaine, Mrs Dright's granddaughter. Elaine beat Emily with such great ease.

Emily got humiliated at losing a game of draughts. The bad loser grabbed hold of a few draughts, then a handful of draughts, and in a tantrum, she dropped them on a chessboard. Emily got off a chair and rose. She made a gesture in anger. She quickly walked out of the room. She did not go back to the drawing-room again. There Elaine played her friend in a game of checkers. Elaine beat her friend again at checkers.

Going back to the living room, Mrs Dright awaited Emily to come. There Emily and Mrs Dright played a game of chess. The marble chess set was a beautiful one. Mrs Dright was a better chess player. Finally, the chess game ended in a stalemate.

After half an hour Mrs Dright had taken more chess pieces and had also dominated the chess game with strategic chess moves. Her chess positions were far more advantageous in attack than her player. Emily resorted to a defensive offensive. A draw was a fair result.

Later, the grandchildren and their friends joined Emily and Mrs Dright in the dining room and they all sat together at the dining table. They drank tea or a glass of milk. They ate sandwiches and a slice of ginger cake. They did like their sweet treat.

Going upstairs to the bathroom, Emily freshened up. Afterwards, she came into a bedroom. Going through the bedroom, she came out through the French doors. There she unexpectedly met Erica waiting for her. Erica moved around the balcony gracefully. Erica sang beautifully, her vocals breathy and passionate.

YOU DANCE FOR ME
In the shadows of the night
You come to me
You dance to me
Dancing to me
In the moonlight, you dance to me

A romanticist deeply in love!

Erica, deeply passionate, made gestures. Erica gesticulated as a singer romantically in love. Emily watched Erica. She was overwhelmed with emotion. She marvelled at her talent for singing.

Going downstairs, Emily stayed till she felt wanted. Her company preferred. The time when she outstayed her welcome, she left immediately. It was her preferable intention to go then, knowing she was unwanted by everybody else.

Emily got into a stagecoach which was about to leave to take her home.

Sitting in the stagecoach, she waved to all of the children waiting outside in the cold along the front of the grounds of the mansion. They shivered. The children stood still as they waved back and breathed in the cold air. Their warm breath rose in the chilly air. They all missed Emily who had departed. They liked their afternoon tea and talking and playing with lady-like Emily, Mrs Dright's favourite person/visitor.

The old widow confided in Emily every time she came to visit her. Mrs Dright spent time reminiscing. Listening to Mrs Dright had interested Emily. Her past as well as her memories were fascinating. Mrs Dright's stories fascinated her.

Chapter 4:

The Lost Memories

Emily dreamt of Grandfather one night. She woke up that morning realising that it was only a dream! She had deep unforgotten memories of her beloved grandfather. She reminisced about her grandfather. She recalled the times she spent with her grandfather when she was only a child, a little girl and a teenager. Grandfather loved Emily. Emily was his favourite granddaughter.

She stayed in the living room and looked at old black and white photographs of Grandfather.

She thought of her past, her memories of Grandfather. Emily mourned for Grandfather. He had been deceased for years.

The only thing she remembered of Grandfather was her good memories. Emily felt deeply saddened when looking at the old photographs. Emily had regrets. She wished she had spent more time with her grandfather. Now it was too late, it was only just sad memories. She remained wistful, pensive and regretful.

Emily did not see the photo album (her mother did not allow her daughter to see it. It's too personal and her mother remained deeply sentimental about it).

Emily still has lost memories.

Chapter 5:

Emily's Memories of Grandfather

Miss Grant came to see her grandmother. Her grandmother made her granddaughter tea. Miss Grant drank the nice tea. It tasted sweet from spoonfuls of sugar.

In the living room, flowers were prettily arranged in ornate vases. Emily admired the flower arrangements and the scent of the fresh flowers.

The son and his wife popped in to see their elderly mother. They had brought round a painting – a countryside landscape.

Their grandmother was ever so fussy about it. Grandmother was affectionately sentimental about it.

Miss Grant thought of Grandfather. She mourned for Grandfather. The granddaughter greatly missed her grandfather. She spoke about her beloved grandfather.

"How long has it been since my grandfather has gone? I really miss my grandfather. I remember when I was a child, I used to go to his big house. My grandfather smoked a pipe. He used to play cribbage. He sat by the fire and told me his stories. I liked to listen to his stories. My grandfather was something of a storyteller. Story-telling was something which he was good at doing."

Sitting on the rocking chair, Grandmother reminisced.

Since a child, Emily enjoyed the amusement pleasure, of her grandfather's story-telling. Emily remembered how her grandfather entertained the grandchildren. The storyteller told them stories.

Grandfather was once a bibliophile. As a bibliomaniac, he was obsessed with bibliomania. Emily remembered that her grandfather would read to her – anything from fiction to classics.

"You do miss your grandfather. I miss him too. He was unwell. You see, he wasn't well. He was a smoker," said Grandmother.

Emily regarded her grandfather with deep affection.

"I do miss my grandfather. I really loved him!"

With deep emotion, Grandmother spoke out. Grandmother was passionately emotional.

"Remember him! Remember the good things about him, not the bad things."

"Oh, I will! He was a good man, a loving father. He was good to me. I miss his story-telling. It's a shame my grandfather was unpublished – his memoirs, journals and those novels of his."

"One day his books will be published," said Grandmother coyly.

"I really do hope so. I hope to see the day."

Emily admired the landscape hung up on the wall. It made a different contrast to everything else, especially the theme. It's a beautiful oil painting. It's beautifully painted with the artist's initials down below. Emily wondered if the painting was safe there. Would it be a target for theft? Perhaps it would get stolen! Emily surmised that the paintings were insured.

Grandmother helped her granddaughter put on her coat.

"Do come again. I will miss you when you go," murmured Grandmother.

"I shan't be long. I won't be gone long. I will miss you too," said Emily disappointedly.

Grandmother escorted her granddaughter out of the front door.

Leaving the Victorian house, Emily got into the stagecoach. Suddenly, at once, the stagecoach left. Emily, seated in the stagecoach, waved goodbye to her grandmother who was standing by the doorway, holding a walking stick. Grandmother was too emotional at watching her granddaughter leave.

Chapter 6:

The Masquerade Invitation (The Last Invite)

On Thursday evening, Emily was together with her friend Lorraine and her elder brother Thomas. Lorraine allowed her brother to stay with them and join in the conversation.

"Aren't you coming to the masquerade?" asked Thomas.

"I don't know. I have been invited, but I am not sure if I want to go," said Emily unsurely.

"Why not? It should be fun. Why don't you? You should have a good time," encouraged Thomas.

"I don't know. All these people going. I don't want to go," said Emily negatively.

Emily still remained doubtful about the masquerade. She had masquerade fears. She panicked. She expected the unexpected.

Lorraine persuaded Emily to change her mind, therefore go to the masquerade.

"Oh, do go! I want you to go. I'll be going. I'll be with you. Don't worry. I'll be there with you," reassured Lorraine.

Emily made her final decision and declined her invitation to the masquerade. She refused as she'd been asked again.

"Not this time. I am not going."

"Why? Oh, please go," implored Lorraine. "I want you to go."

Emily was reluctant and half-hearted about going to the masquerade.

"Don't force me to go. I will think about it."

Lorraine stepped back. Lorraine made gestures. Lorraine disapproved of Emily's lack of enthusiasm for going to the masquerade.

"Oh, go on! Do go!" prompted Lorraine.

Emily felt pressure as her friend prompted her. Emily wrote on a scrap of paper unconditionally: "You do have my word."

Emily decided to go. She agreed to attend this year's masquerade. She signed it indefinitely. She appeared to be quite enthusiastic about going to the masquerade. Emily was half-hearted at attending the masquerade whilst her friend was wholehearted about going to the masquerade. Emily expected full attendance at the masquerade ball. It pleased her very much that she had female company, a chaperone. The camaraderie was certainly pleasing.

In a few months, there was a masquerade, unless of course it was cancelled until further notice.

Emily dreaded it, while her friend Lorraine looked forward to it with interest.

On a calendar, Emily counted down the days left before the masquerade.

Chapter 7:

Strangers and Masqueraders Leave the Masquerade

At the masquerade, there were about a hundred guests, masqueraders. Emily sat in a room with other guests – strangers.

Lorraine was impatient at having to wait until 7.45 P.M. At that time, they both left the sitting room to go to the ballroom. They did not recognise the masked masqueraders. All the masqueraders were disguised. Those acquaintances and strangers were unrecognisable wearing masks. A masquerade pretence.

Those that were invited were friends of Quentin Burrows, the host, a squire.

The orchestra played chamber music. All of the masked masqueraders danced, male and female. Emily joined Lorraine somewhere on the ballroom floor. They danced with every masquerader. Emily took comfort in wearing a mask. Her disguised identity was unrevealed.

The masqueraders danced beautifully well, with such dignified grace. The pace was slow and quick. The movements were slow and the pace quickened.

Suddenly, a masquerader, a stranger, came forward. The male masquerader was masked. The masquerader was mischievous, sly and pretentious. Emily wooed the masquerader by dancing gracefully. She attracted him. The enamoured masquerader reacted in deep love, desiring her. Emily was overwhelmed with emotional love and strong desire.

As the music ended, so the dance ended. At that time, both Emily and the male masquerader left the crowded ballroom, going out of the double doors. Revealing his identity, Emily swooned at the married man. Emily desired him. A handsome aristocrat.

Suddenly, the wife grabbed hold of her husband and led him away outside the front drive of the grand stately home.

Emily was stranded, watching them. Quickly, the husband and wife got into a stagecoach. The married couple were quickly driven away in the pitch dark night.

Lorraine ran out and re-joined Emily, standing by a street lamp.

"Who is he?" asked Lorraine.

Emily put her hand on her heart. Her heart was beating.

"I don't know. He's the sweetest and cutest man I ever did see," sighed Emily.

"Is he married?" asked Lorraine.

"I don't know if the stranger is married. He must be. There was a gold wedding ring on his finger," paused Emily. "Did you see that masquerader staring at me?"

"Who was it? Didn't they all stare at you?"

"It was that girl, silly," Emily blurted out.

"What girl?"

Emily remained reticent as she became heartrendingly emotional as well as upset too.

Going back indoors, Emily lost the pleasure of excitement. It remained a disenchantment for the rest of the night.

Feeling disappointed, Emily kept her mask on as a precaution.

Emily left the masquerade with her invited friend. They were the next ones to leave the masquerade. They feared the mist happening at any time tonight, a possible misty night.

Getting into a stagecoach, they both set off on their journey home, waving goodbye to the enchanted masqueraders walking outside in the grounds. The masqueraders reacted by waving goodbye. On their enchanting masked faces, their bewitching smiles charmed them.

From a fountain, jets of water emanated out. It sparkled in the glorious light. They were both spellbound by the haunting night.

Chapter 8:

Emily's Reflection on the Girl

Going into the garden, Emily and Lorraine found Thomas using a hose to water the garden thoroughly. Finding themselves intruded on, they went inside the greenhouse. Here they had privacy until Thomas intruded on them. They took discomfort from claustrophobia. There were many potted plants everywhere.

They decided to go back indoors. They went into the lounge. Emily closed the door behind her.

"Did you see that girl?" asked Emily.

"Do you mean the girl dressed up as a peacock?"

"How do you know it's her?" doubted Lorraine.

Emily raised her tone of voice.

"It was the same girl. I am telling you."

"What's her name?" asked Lorraine.

"I don't know her name. She's a complete stranger."

"You don't know her name. No one seems to know the stranger," said Lorraine, baffled.

Remembering the masquerade, Emily was puzzled at all the disguised masqueraders and their unrevealed identities.

"I could not recognise them."

Lorraine was baffled at the masked masqueraders too. Lorraine didn't recognise them. Lorraine was perplexed.

"Neither could I recognise them."

"The masquerade was strange. It was weird and wonderful. It was enchanting," remarked Emily.

"It was quite wonderful, bizarre and enchanting," commented Lorraine.

Standing by the door, Thomas eavesdropped. He opened the door and came in. He imposed on them after eavesdropping earlier.

"Why didn't you invite me?" said Brother agitatedly.

"You have been listening. Next time, maybe next time," said Sister undoubtedly.

"I would love to come," said Brother eagerly.

"I know, dear boy. Enough said about it," said Sister abruptly.

Emily refused to express herself by blabbing. She kept quiet. She smirked with childish mischievousness.

Emily and Lorraine went upstairs. Emily went into Lorraine's bedroom, with Lorraine joining her. Alone together, they resumed their conversation, both friends intimate as they confided together.

"What do you know about this girl?" asked Lorraine.

Answering the question, Emily blabbed out, "She's emotional. She plays the guitar. She's poetical. She writes her own lyrics."

"Does she? That's really interesting. I would like to see and hear her play," said Lorraine curiously.

"Will I ever see her again? I don't know," said Emily doubtfully.

"She's a mystery!"

Lorraine doubted. Lorraine had a difference of opinion.

"How do you know these things?" asked Lorraine.

"The witch told me," replied Emily. "The white witch offered to read my palm. I refused."

"I don't blame you. I would do the same thing."

Emily thought of the occult, the clandestine imagery.

"I am not interested in the crystal ball and black cat."

"It is better for us not to dabble in it. Stick with the church, I say."

"We are churchgoers. We are proper madams," chuckled Emily.

"I like to wear Sunday best, don't you? And then there's Sunday School."

"Those were the days; discipline and strict upbringing," recalled Emily.

"What I would say about you, is that you have morals. You are moralistic."

"I try not to sin. Sinning – isn't sin the way of the world?" said Emily philosophically.

Lorraine seemed to be confessional regarding committing sin.

"You're a good person. My sins are big. I am a sinner. Crikey! I am a materialist. I am sinful!" Lorraine confessed.

"It doesn't have to be that way. If one repents, your sins are washed away."

"Coming from you, you are a fine example," praised Lorraine.

Emily stayed with Lorraine until it was eventually time to leave to go home.

At home, Emily lounged about in a restful, relaxed manner, thinking of the masquerade and that mysterious girl whom she had had the pleasure of meeting. She wondered if she would ever meet the girl again. She hoped she would see and meet her again. She was saddened at not seeing her again. Emily had become quite attached to the girl.

Chapter 9:

A Deeper Understanding of Ginger

With intimate togetherness, Emily confided in Lorraine. Keeping warm while sitting near the fireplace, they both warmed up in the warmth of the room.

"What else happened to the girl?" asked Lorraine.

"I saw the girl hold an old photo."

"Who was it?"

"The girl's aunt. Her aunt abandoned her. The girl was distraught. The girl showed a photo. No one could help her in her time of crisis. It was a lost cause. Her aunt emigrated to Canada. Her aunt lived her new life over there. The truth is, the girl hated her aunt! She didn't care about her aunt anymore. Her sympathetic mother showed sympathy," responded Emily.

Emily recalled the enchanting masquerade. She felt enchanted. Her memories of the masquerade were a thrill of enchantment.

"I did see the girl. I didn't really pay much attention. Other things took my interest. I was distracted by other things."

"At first I didn't pay any attention to the sad girl," said Emily admittedly.

"It was unfortunate what happened. It gave me cause for concern. I couldn't do anything to help her," said Lorraine.

"The girl was neglected. All alone. It was totally unacceptable. I took her back to her mother. I complained about it," recalled Emily.

"The others seemed to agree. Her mother did not neglect her daughter anymore," remembered Lorraine.

"The girl was looking for love. I attended to her at the right time. I am so glad I did. The girl reacted to my love. She responded to my love. Ginger felt much better the moment she left," sighed Emily.

"Poor child! I hope she gets over it," said Lorraine sympathetically.

"Me too. I hope she recovers. The sooner the better."

During one of the masquerades, Emily and Lorraine had such thoughtfulness for the unloved girl, neglected and unattended. They showed consideration for the relieved girl, who exited out of the manor house with her parents.

It was a triumphant departure, to those saying and waving goodbye to them both. As the stagecoach was going down through the grounds, the guests acknowledged them as they waved goodbye for the final time.

Chapter 10:

The Picnic

Emily wrote to Ginger. They agreed to meet up. They arranged a place, time and date. (The witch gave Emily the girl's address.)

On a Saturday afternoon, Emily met Ginger at a picnic spot within an area of a beauty spot. Emily waited near the seating area. Emily was wrapped up. She was calm and peaceful at having the opportunity to meet Ginger.

Ginger met Emily on time. Emily was pleased to meet Ginger. Ginger wore a coat, gloves and a hat.

"Hello, Ginger. It's good to meet you. Thank you for coming," greeted Emily.

"Thank you for coming. It's a pleasure to meet you. What do you think of the location?"

Emily marvelled at the surroundings, the conservation environment.

"It's lovely and romantic here. It's quite different to anywhere else."

Ginger smiled. Ginger unbuttoned her coat. She wore a necklace.

Emily noticed the silver necklace. She saw the stunning silver necklace and a brooch. The gem, an emerald, sparkled.

"I love your silver chain. Where did you get it from?" asked Emily.

"My father bought it for me," replied Ginger.

"Oh! How nice. It's lovely."

"My father buys me jewellery," lied Ginger.

"Do you have lots of jewels?" asked Emily.

"I have a fair share of jewels. How about you?"

"I do have jewellery. Some of it is hand-me-down jewels," answered Emily.

Ginger acknowledged her family trait. Her grandmother's obsessional possession of jewels.

"I do too."

"Is everything better at home?" wondered Emily.

In her state of mind, Ginger remained reticent. Ginger denied having abundant possession of jewellery.

"Everything is alright," said Ginger curtly.

Emily and Ginger walked past the few picnickers sitting in the fields eating their picnic. They enjoyed their stroll along the beauty spot. The natural sight was naturally breath-taking. They admired and marvelled at the beautiful countryside.

Emily and Ginger stopped when they came to remote fields. There they put their bag and wicker basket. They lay on a spread blanket. There they both enjoyed having a picnic. (In June, the summer weather is hotter.)

They ate a sandwich each and drank cordial and ginger ale. It was such a romantic picnic spot. A beautiful sunshiny spot. A beamy radiance.

During that time, the picnickers remained silent. They marvelled at the natural beauty spot. They admired the natural wonder of beauty. On their first outing together, they enjoyed themselves. It was a wonderful summer's day.

***

As Emily reached home, she read the newspaper headlines:

WATCH OUT! MORE BURGLARIES IN AREA.

Emily paid attention to the newspaper and within moments she discarded the newspaper.

Mrs Grant was agitated with her daughter.

"Keep the windows locked and closed. Don't open the windows," reprimanded Mother.

Emily had serious thoughts of burglary. She wondered if their house was a target for burglary. There had been certain houses burgled in the area.

Emily felt rather tired after the picnic and from travelling home. Today, she had a lovely picnic alone with her new friend.

Emily stayed in her bedroom. She lay down on her bed and rested.

Her mother took the necessary precautions regarding security. Emily was worried about her home being burgled. She took precautions by locking her valuables in a safe. They both regained reassurance from security. It made a difference by taking security measures. They got security and peace of mind from protective measures.

Chapter 11:

The Letters

On a cold Sunday evening, Emily stayed in. She did not go to church today. Emily was usually punctual with her church attendance every Sunday. Instead, Emily wrote a letter to Ginger:

Dear Ginger,

I am writing to you, my friend. It is a joy to know you. I hope you are keeping well. I hope you get over your problems. I am a churchgoer myself. Going to church helps me. It reassures me at times. My spiritual life is good!

All that fellowship and having faith do make things much better. Quite recently I have been distressed. There have been more burglaries in the area. I am worried and fearful of us being burgled next. My mother agitates me, telling me to wise up. She tells me to lock the windows and doors. My mother locks up her valuables in a safe and I lock my bedroom. We are concerned about burglaries. The neighbours are vigilant. They keep a watch-out! The neighbours suspect. We don't want our house to be burgled. We take the necessary precautions. We want security. We want to live in peace and safety. My mum says it's life! It's one of those things you have to deal with. This fear/phobia has made me down to earth. I am not a materialist. I am not obsessional about materialism. In fact, I am casual about worldly things. I am not obsessive about materialism. But everything is ordinary to me. I have a casual approach to materialistic things.

I had to write to you to express my concerns.

Yours sincerely,

Emily.

Ginger wrote:

Dear Emily,

I am sorry you are having problems with burglaries in your area. I too have the same problem. My precious jewels!

I have a lot of jewellery. I am obsessed with jewellery. Just like my grandmother.

Do take precautions. Then everything will be alright.

My mother is a snob! I try to be down to earth. I have learned that most things are unimportant. Having faith is far more important in life.

Do write. We must meet up again.

Love,

Ginger.

Chapter 12:

The Accusation

Ginger invited Emily to High Downe with her mother. Ginger had high tea. Emily welcomed the warm invitation.

Whilst handing a teacup and a saucer to Emily, Emily noticed Ginger's arm was grazed. She caught sight of Ginger's graze.

"How did you do that?" asked Emily.

"I fell over," replied Ginger.

"You really must be careful. You'll hurt yourself," said Emily.

"You stupid girl!" said Mother.

"I fall down, but I don't hurt myself like that," simpered Emily.

"My dear! You are careful. That's what *you* should be."

"I do try. I am reckless," said Ginger.

Ginger looked at her left arm. She fretted at the sight of it.

"You needn't worry. It will be alright."

"My love! You're supple," remarked Mother.

"Not really. Just stupid," admitted Ginger.

"How you crawl through holes, I don't know," said Emily curiously.

"My dear sweet father is not around. Father's at work. A printer."

"You miss your father," said Mother.

"Father works late nights," murmured Ginger.

Emily was surprised that Ginger wore no jewellery. Her fingers were ringless. Ginger wore no ring on her ring finger. Emily envied Ginger's obsessive possession of fine jewels. Ginger's tendency for possession. Obsessiveness was an obsession!

"Where were you last night?" asked Mother.

"I was at my friend's," answered Daughter.

"That explains the graze."

"I fell over and hurt myself."

After tea, Ginger took Emily alone to her bedroom. There, on the dressing table, Ginger took out a ruby ring from her jewellery box. Ginger showed her most favourite jewel. Ginger was obsessional about her possessions, especially her ruby ring for which she had deep sentimentality, also a fondness and sentimental love. She deeply felt for her grandmother.

A few days later, Ginger found that her ruby ring had been stolen from her jewellery box. Ginger accused her mother of stealing her ruby ring. Ginger's mother strongly denied it, the absurd allegation. Did Ginger's mother begrudge her daughter? Begrudging her daughter, Ginger's grandmother gave her granddaughter a gift!

The next afternoon, Emily met Ginger at High Downe.

Ginger confided in Emily. "My mother did it! Who else?" snapped Ginger.

"It's likely your mother did it. Your mother's bloody awful!"

"My mother denies it," said Ginger.

"Perhaps your mother begrudges you, your grandmother for giving you a gift."

"Perhaps my mother does begrudge me. I hate her. Why does my mother do this to me?"

"Your mother begrudges you. She really does."

"My father is unconcerned. He doesn't want to be burdened with problems," said Ginger.

"You're going through an awful time. Do take care. Beware of thieves!" said Emily.

"It's my favourite ring. It has sentimental value," frowned Ginger.

"Your grandmother gave it to you as a gift!"

Ginger sulked. The girl was a sulker.

"My things were stolen."

Emily offered Ginger advice. Emily suggested: "You should hide it away!"

"I have no other alternative but to do so."

Ginger agreed to hide away her jewellery. It was the safest option.

Emily, deeply concerned for Ginger, decided to leave High Downe.

Ginger neglected Emily. Emily unappreciated her thoughtlessness.

Chapter 13:

The Stolen Jewels

Mr and Mrs Grant spoke to Mrs Snowdon, a neighbour. They imposed on her. Mrs Snowden was deeply concerned about the neighbours' houses being burgled. The vigilant neighbours were on a neighbourhood watch. The neighbours were vigilant, belligerent and intimidating. They disliked the idea of certain neighbours being victims of burglaries.

Emily enquired about Mrs Snowdon's involvement with the neighbourhood watch. The neighbours again had been watchful.

"What happened yesterday?" enquired Emily.

"My friend and neighbour's house was burgled," replied Mother.

"How was it done?" asked Emily.

"There was a break-in. The burglars broke in through a sash window," replied Mother.

"What was stolen?"

"The house was ransacked. Jewellery was stolen."

"It's the same thing. The same crime. Were there any clues?" asked Emily.

"No there weren't. It was a small window. Someone small broke in."

"It's the same old story. It's the same burglar," said Emily conclusively.

"We don't know. Your guess is as good as ours," said Mother unsurely.

"My hunch is it's the same burglar doing it. Sooner or later the burglar will be caught!" said Emily undoubtedly.

"What's the motive?" asked Mother.

"I don't know. It's some obsession of some sort."

"It's a crime. The neighbours go berserk, carrying bats and knives."

"It's crazy!" muttered Emily.

Emily thought of Mrs Snowdon's explanation. According to her, it's an unsolved crime.

"Who do you think it is?" asked Mother.

"It must be a gang or something. Maybe it's the same burglar? It's the same thing. A break-in through a window. Stolen jewellery. That sort of thing. I have my doubts and suspicions. Whoever is the suspect is likely to be the culprit. Whichever is the burglar, thief?"

A concentrating Emily contemplated crime. Her contemplation on was solved and unsolved crime. She could not explain the cause of the burglaries. Emily was perplexed by a coincidental Saturday night break-in.

Every night there had been a full moon when the thief struck! In different areas, every house had been burgled. From subsequent burglaries theft occurred. The most common thing taken was jewels. There were jewels stolen in abundance.

Ginger came to the party. Ginger was the last one to enter the manor house. The guest was enigmatic, strange and mysterious. Ginger wore a black dress and a necklace. (Her beloved grandmother gave her granddaughter a gift.)

The obsessive admirers obsessed over Ginger. They desired and fancied her.

Emily thought of Ginger as being pretentious, elegant, sophisticated and debonair. Her sophistication and mannerisms were like that of a classy lady. Ginger was a proud urchin! Her elegance was lady-like and her grace nymph-like.

Emily noticed Ginger had been escorted and accompanied out of a room. An admirer danced with Ginger in the ballroom. Ginger was elated and euphoric. She might have been triumphant! Tonight was the best night of her life!

Ginger was dancing with someone who she desired. The admirer admired, adored and loved her. The host, Mr and Mrs Burrows' son.

Emily hadn't seen Ginger for a long time. She realised Ginger was having a good time at the party. Ginger hadn't missed Emily's presence or company.

Emily had forgotten that Ginger existed. Ginger's presence was more like an absence. Ginger wasn't present anywhere, only in the ballroom when Ginger danced.

Guests remarked and commented more on Ginger than anybody else. Emily envied Ginger. Emily, lost for words, had wondered about Ginger. Emily did not dance. She talked to guests. She stayed in the living room to suit herself, talking to ladies and gentlemen. These individuals made a fuss of Emily. Emily liked the attention she received. However, she had been eclipsed throughout the night. The fascination with an eclipse in the skies.

Ginger, adored and liked, had received all the attention. Ginger enjoyed her time with the one whom she deeply loved. They paid attention to Ginger. Her attentiveness and alertness in a virginal bridal suit.

Emily had met some of the Englishwomen. They were bejewelled. They were adorned with jewellery. Ginger was attracted by the sight of their jewels. Ginger wanted to rob them. Ginger was favoured by the host. Mr and Mrs Burrows adored Ginger. Their son loved Ginger. Ginger spent time with Mr and Mrs Burrows' son. Ginger had been uninterested in everything else.

Emily, talking to others, was unable to talk to Ginger. Ginger avoided and eluded Emily on purpose. Ginger's intention was deliberate to keep away from Emily.

For hours Emily kept away from Ginger. This party was strange. It was full of guests who were strangers. (A gate-crasher attended.)

Emily felt uneasy in the presence and company of strangers. She was already acquainted with some guests. The other guests were loquacious.

Emily remained in a strange frame of mind. She had been unsociable and silent. Emily left the party when she felt unwanted and unloved by everybody else.

Leaving the manor house, she hurried into a stagecoach which took her home. The journey was long. A long night.

Chapter 14:

Emily Alone with Ginger

At High Downe, Emily spent time with Ginger. Emily was pent up at not having seen Ginger for a few days. With deep emotion, Emily had been passionate.

"I have missed you. I am glad to be with you again."

"Emily, I have missed you. It's only been a few days since I last saw you."

"I didn't see you much at the party. It was a real shame."

"I was with Mr and Mrs Burrows' son," replied Ginger.

"That must have been romantic."

"Oh, it was a good romance," smiled Ginger.

Emily recalled. The observer took note.

"You were so occupied with him that nothing else really mattered."

"I was in love! It was more like a crush rather than a love."

Emily changed the topic.

"Did you hear about the lady? Her jewels were pinched," said Emily.

"Such an awful shame."

"Where were you?" asked Emily.

"I was with Mr and Mrs Burrows' son."

"How did the woman lose them?" asked Emily.

"I don't know. She must have been careless," replied Ginger.

"Was she the only one who lost her jewels?"

"She must have been the only one."

"The woman reported it to the police."

"The police didn't do much."

"Do you have a lead?"

"That the motive is jewels!"

"The women did wear lovely jewels."

"They did. I wore my grandmother's necklace."

"Oh you did, did you?"

Ginger twirled her finger around her silver necklace.

"I love it!"

Emily noted Ginger's obsessive tendency.

"You have lots of jewels."

Ginger was not ashamed of her obsessive possession of jewels, her jewellery obsession and obsessiveness.

"Everybody was having a good time. Theft was the last thing on their minds," remarked Ginger.

"It didn't seem possible," said Emily.

"Most of the women wore jewellery. They weren't troubled."

"One of the women got robbed," mentioned Emily.

"Oh, she did? Oh, how unfortunate!"

Drinking tea, Emily and Ginger sat down together. They both relived their highlights of the party. They had such good memories.

The next day, Emily visited Mrs Dright. Mrs Dright questioned Emily about the peculiar girl. Mrs Dright had serious concerns. Emily seemed unconcerned.

"Ginger's my friend."

"She is strange. Where does Ginger get all that jewellery from?" muttered Mrs Dright.

Her grandmother gave it to her," answered Emily.

"That spoilt child! She's got too much," grumbled Mrs Dright.

The sympathiser showed sympathy.

"Ginger does suffer. I care about her. It won't stop me from loving her," said Emily affectionately.

"Quite frankly, miss, you are gullible."

"I love Ginger. We are good friends," smiled Emily.

"She's bad!"

"On the contrary. Ginger is a dear, sweet friend," defended Emily.

Mrs Dright criticised Ginger. "Ginger needs to be punished. She's bad for you."

"I understand your concern. Ginger is carefree, easy-going and laid-back. Ginger won't change."

"Ginger has got too much. She needs punishment," said Mrs Dright unsympathetically.

Emily's views differed from Mrs Dright's. She defended Ginger passionately.

"I like Ginger. She's a nice girl. She needs love. I love her."

Emily outstayed her welcome. Her brief visit was short. She left Mrs Dright's mansion, taking the stagecoach to get home. Her journey home was long. Today was a sunny day with fine weather.

Chapter 15: Girl Friday

Emily waited for Lorraine to get home. She spent time talking to Thomas in the lounge. Lorraine's younger brother was good-looking, exuberant, nice and pleasant.

"How is Ginger?" asked Thomas.

"Ginger is well. She collects jewellery in a jam jar," replied Emily.

Ginger's strangeness and mysteriousness perplexed Thomas.

"Where does Ginger get it all from?" paused Thomas. "Ginger has lots of jewellery."

Emily responded, "Ginger's grandmother has plenty of jewellery. Her grandmother gives it to her granddaughter."

"How have you been?" asked Thomas.

"I have been alright. I have been housebound these days, I suppose due to the increase in burglaries. I have spent my days indoors. My mother mixes with the neighbours. We are vigilantes. We are watchful of our neighbourhood. We barricade our doors," said Emily defiantly.

"Oh, that! We are alright. It hasn't affected us," gasped Thomas.

"Ginger is concerned about the burglaries. It has affected her. Her mother is protective."

Waiting for Lorraine, Emily was inclined to be conversational. The topic which arose remained controversial. Emily talked about burglaries.

Arriving home, Lorraine greeted Emily, coming home from work after the typist had finished her secretarial work and administrative duties.

"Do lock up," urged Emily.

"You too must take caution. Do beware," said Lorraine cautiously.

Lorraine, wanting her privacy, preferred to be alone, desiring to reflect on her romance. Lorraine was filled with romantic excitement.

Lorraine set a date in her diary when she would next meet Emily.

Emily embraced Lorraine and her affectionate brother before leaving to go home. Emily walked home in the drizzle. The distance back to her house was considerably longer on foot.

Emily reached her house. Her mother was waiting outside for her daughter. Mrs Grant was agitated with her daughter. With a key, Mrs Grant opened the front door, allowing her daughter to come in first through the front door.

"Lock up the doors and windows," demanded Mother.

Emily understood the situation. She realised the serious importance of it.

"Yes, Mom," obeyed Daughter.

They both felt safer from taking security measures. Their house was safe from burglars. They felt reassured from taking caution. They were both unafraid. Without fears and anxieties, both mother and daughter slept peacefully that night. A peaceful night.

Chapter 16:

The Burglary

The burglar sneaked into the back garden. There the burglar took off the pole which raised the washing line. The burglar used the pole to smash the pane of a window. The burglar broke in. The burglar ransacked the house. On a dressing table, there was a jewellery box. Lorraine's jewellery was stolen.

Hours later Lorraine and her parents came home from the restaurant. They found their house had been burgled. It was a complete shock to them. Nothing else was taken, only Lorraine's jewellery.

Thomas offered comfort to his sister. He consoled his sister. Thomas was sympathetic. The brother was sympathetically sweet to his sister. Thomas double-checked the jewellery box.

"It's all gone," said Brother.

"What am I going to do? My jewels are all gone!"

Thomas tried to offer comfort to his sister.

Lorraine burst out in tears.

"My jewels! It's gone!"

Lorraine came out into the garden alone. She whispered:

My heart is broken.

My heart aches.

Thomas comforted his sister. Lorraine was shocked and deeply upset and miserable and sad. She cried. Lorraine was shocked by the shocking experience. How would Lorraine overcome the trauma of burglary? The theft of her precious jewels?

Sara, one of Lorraine's friends, informed Emily of the burglary at Lorraine's house. Emily came right away to see her distressed friend.

At Lorraine's house, Emily listened intently to Lorraine as she retraced yesterday night.

Emily offered help and comfort to Lorraine. Lorraine broke down. Lorraine's considerate friend was thoughtful and deeply sympathetic. The sympathiser was comforting, sympathetic and accommodating.

Emily spent time with Lorraine. Her friend was deeply distressed. Emily offered her friend Lorraine help, support and advice. Emily consoled and comforted Lorraine. She slipped one of her rings on Lorraine's finger.

Lorraine took comfort from Emily. Lorraine appreciated her thoughtful friend's love.

Chapter 17:

Mrs Grant's Deep Concerns

After coming home from Lorraine's house, Emily entered the lounge. She slouched on a sofa. She was deeply troubled. Emily worried about Lorraine. Her mother showed deep concern.

"What happened? How is Lorraine?" asked Mother.

"Lorraine is in a bad state. She's distressed. Her jewels were stolen. I don't think she will ever get over the theft."

Mrs Grant noticed her daughter's finger was ringless. Mrs Grant's ring finger had a wedding ring.

"Where's your ring?" asked Mother.

"I gave it to Lorraine," replied Emily.

"You shouldn't be giving your ring away," admonished Mother.

"I don't have any regrets. I felt I *had* to give my ring away. At least I have given solace to Lorraine, I have given her some comfort."

"How is Lorraine's mother and Thomas?" asked Mother.

"They have taken it badly. They are still in a state of shock," answered Daughter.

"What was taken?" asked Mother.

"The only thing taken was Lorraine's jewels. It's strange! Nothing else was taken."

"A jewel thief. It's the most common thing stolen," said Mother.

Emily expressed her fears.

"We might be next. We have to take caution. We have to be vigilant," said Emily apprehensively.

Mrs Grant expressed her concerns.

"We will have to barricade. We will have to lock up."

"We do indeed."

"Won't Mrs Bridges consider selling up?"

"Mom, I don't know. The thought has crossed my mind."

"Don't keep jewels! It will get stolen! It will be a target," said Mother cautiously.

"Everything will be stolen in a flash."

"I have notified the police," informed Mother.

"They won't do anything," tutted Daughter.

Emily was feeling tired from travelling. She left her mother, who was deep in thought contemplating burglary.

Going to her bedroom, Emily lay down on her bed and rested. She contemplated theft, wondering about what sort of measure to take against theft. Emily was apprehensive due to all the burglaries in the neighbourhood. She remained fearful.

Going to Sunday School today, Emily and Ginger left together for the church service to attend to the children attending Sunday School.

Two of the girls wore jewellery. They learned about Noah's Ark.

"You won't take their jewellery, will you?" said Emily provocatively.

"No, of course not. What makes you think that? I won't do that. Never do that," said Ginger seriously.

Together, the good children learned about the Old Testament. They were deeply spiritual and biblical. One of the children's parents were Christians, Pentecostals, and the other parents are regular churchgoers, Pentecostals.

In the church building, the children were taught. Emily and Ginger were helpers. Crèche took place as well on the same day.

Chapter 18:

The Watchful Neighbours

During the course of weeks, Lorraine joined the neighbourhood watch. The neighbours would join up altogether. They belonged to the neighbourhood watch.

At one neighbour's house, Lorraine and Emily joined up. They stood by the window and kept watch. Everything seemed normal as usual. There wasn't anything to report as suspicious. The neighbours observed people walking by and the cyclists riding. A gentleman in a bowler hat was walking with his umbrella.

The observant neighbours from other houses noticed watchful neighbours keeping watch. The neighbours were alert, vigil and vigilant. Anything suspicious, they had reported. The neighbours discussed the trend of burglaries, how it arose, and how the neighbourhood watch could stamp out burglaries.

The neighbours agreed on 'positional strategies': to report and alert the police of anything suspicious in the area and the neighbourhood.

Lorraine was wrathful. She wanted revenge. She took a positive approach to the neighbourhood watch. Lorraine joined the neighbourhood watch because of personal reasons. Furthermore, her mother forced her to join against her will.

The results were positive. There was a reduction in burglaries due to ongoing neighbourhood watch. Every neighbour in the group was afraid of their house getting burgled, so they all took precautions. As a result, taking cautionary measures. The neighbours were reassured by the watch. They gained confidence and reassurance from the burglaries being reduced.

They each took turns to keep watch. The neighbours came together and met up to discuss the prevention of crime and break-ins.

The neighbours implemented the following strategies: keeping watch around the clock, and reporting any suspicious activity. Regularly, the neighbours watched, reported, informed and alerted the police. The constable attended to their needs. Every neighbour in the group felt much safer because of the security. All the neighbours took the necessary caution required. They all rested assured.

Subsequently, in the area, there was a decrease and a reduction in burglaries. From the campaign, there was a positive result.

Chapter 19:

The Chance Meeting

Lorraine and her brother came to see Emily at her house. Emily was pleased to meet them. She warmly welcomed them. They still suffered from the trauma of the burglary. Lorraine suffered deeply from affliction.

They sat down in the lounge. Emily caught sight of Lorraine's gold ring.

"You're so kind. I shan't forget it. You're a love. I treasure it with my heart," said Lorraine appreciatively.

Emily was thrilled with joy in giving Lorraine her ring.

"I am glad you like it."

Lorraine, sitting on a chair, had admired her ring.

"Like it? Love it!" exclaimed Lorraine admirably.

"My sister loves your ring," said Thomas joyously.

Lorraine acknowledged her state.

"I am suffering. You giving me your ring has made all the difference. It has given me solace and made me feel better from your love."

"How is the watch?" asked Emily.

"The watch is really important to us. I must emphasise it. We realise the importance of it. My jewels were stolen. It has shaken me up. I will never get over the theft, losing my jewels. I guess now we have the benefit of the watch. We feel safer and reassured. It is a deterrent, a crackdown on crime. As neighbours, we came together. We can discuss things, we can take action, we can report anything suspicious, our observations," said Lorraine frankly.

Thomas thought of the benefit of the neighbourhood watch, and how essential it was. It was crucial in effect!

"It is good for us to keep watch. We can keep an eye out. We can take caution. We can act now," said Thomas assuredly.

"Our mother shouts at us. She insists on the watch, going out to the neighbourhood watch," frowned Lorraine.

"We haven't regretted it. It's a good, positive thing. We learn about crime. We educate ourselves to fight crime, to tackle crime, by taking measures against crime."

"The ladies like a chinwag, to get down to the nitty-gritty," grinned Lorraine.

Emily was fatalistic. She dreaded the worst happening. She was fearful and apprehensive of being burgled, being a victim of crime.

"Our mother insists on us doing a neighbourhood watch. That way it will prevent crime, protect us from crime," said Emily assertively.

"You should do it, you know, for your sakes," said Lorraine unashamedly.

"You should join up before it's too late," insisted Thomas.

"You should, you know. Why don't you? It is a good thing. We shall see the results," encouraged Lorraine.

Thomas looked around the room. He admired the antiques and ornaments and from the cabinet the fine set of crockery.

"You have got some fine things here. You should take note of all the break-ins," warned Thomas.

Suffering from fear and anxiety, Emily and her mother, who came into the room, both decided to join a neighbourhood watch. The others belonged to one. They felt much better at joining a group. They would take measures against having a burglary any time now, or any day and night now. Their house may be the next target. Emily and her mother took necessary caution by using a deterrent to deter.

Leaving the house, Lorraine and her brother went home.

Emily and her mother made sure everything was locked up securely.

Lorraine belonged to a neighbourhood watch group. She got counselling. A disturbed young woman!

Her brother was indurated, rebellious, violent and defiant.

Emily and her mother joined a neighbourhood watch scheme.

Ginger gave up being a jewel thief! Stealing did remain a temptation of hers!

Ginger was reformed, regenerated and converted!

Ginger was a helper at Sunday School. Ginger attended to the children attending.

Ginger was blessed!

Chapter 20:

Ginger Almost Makes a Confession

One night, Ginger burst into the room. In the room, seated, were Emily, Thomas and his sister Lorraine. Ginger had an urge to confess, therefore to make a confession.

"I didn't mean it. I didn't mean to do it," said Ginger apologetically.

"Do what?" said Emily.

"What's wrong?" said Lorraine.

"You haven't done anything wrong."

"Well then," they said.

Not making a confessionary response, Ginger kept silent.

One by one, Emily, Lorraine and Thomas held Ginger's hand. By squeezing it passionately, their touch passionate, the sympathisers emotional. Ginger was overwhelmed with emotion. Ginger felt remorse. The remorseful girl showed repentance for her misdeed!

That winter's night, Ginger left Emily's house (a target for burglary!) at once. Ginger was feeling much better after having not quite confessed and not admitted. Ginger survived another day without imprisonment!

Ginger came to see Emily at her house. Ginger came at a time when Mrs Grant had gone out late in the day. Emily was alone with Ginger. Ginger was well-behaved, reserved and deeply contemplative.

"You really should be safe here. There won't be any burglaries," said Ginger self-assuredly.

"I hope not. The burglars won't get away with it. The police will close in. What will you do with all your jewels?" muttered Emily.

"I will keep them. I will treasure it. It belonged to my late grandmother," answered Ginger.

Emily came forward to Ginger who was standing still. Ginger stayed calm and cool. Ginger took off a ring from her finger. Ginger slipped a ring onto Emily's finger.

"There! You can have it. A gift from me to you."

Emily was deeply appreciative of having been given a ring. Emily treasured it from her heart of hearts. She had a deep love for Ginger. A great love!

Chapter 21:

The Crime in Society

At the neighbourhood watch, Emily spent time with the neighbours keeping watch. They watched out for anything suspicious. (Lorraine and her mother already belonged to a neighbourhood watch group.)

In the meantime, Emily and her mother joined a neighbourhood watch group, therefore, to deter from having a burglary. They knew their house would be burgled next. It was inevitable!

The neighbours kept watch. Subsequently, they reported and informed the police accordingly, looking out for anything suspicious. With the neighbourhood watch keeping watch, it may have resulted in a crackdown on crime. It diminished.

Joining and belonging to a neighbourhood watch, none of them was any longer a target for burglary. The threat of it was less likely in society today.

Nowadays, the neighbourhood watch groups are vigilant, safe and protected. It deters and prevents break-ins and crime.

As a result of crime in society, the police educate the community, as well as schools and institutes etc.

Regularly, the neighbourhood watch keeps watch usually to deter burglaries and prevent crime. They look out for burglars. The neighbours, in anticipation, expect burglars to burgle at random.

The watchful neighbours were alert (the neighbourhood watch joined up. They kept a watch-out). They reported and informed the police. In certain areas, break-ins were becoming fewer and fewer in neighbourhoods. In some parts of Britain, committed crime was on the increase.

Chapter 22:

Ginger's Conversion

One afternoon at Emily's snug house, Emily confronted Ginger. Emily suspected Ginger as the burglar, the thief!

Emily and Ginger stayed for some time in the sitting room. The spacious room was quieter, cooler and shadier.

Emily stood beside Ginger who was laid-back, calm, unperturbed and peaceful. Her disposition a serenity.

"Why did you do it?" said Emily.

"Do what?"

"Steal the jewels, burgle the houses," said Emily allegedly.

"I don't know what you're talking about," objected Ginger.

"Oh, come on! It's you, isn't it!" suspected Emily.

Standing, Ginger looked at the broad daylight coming through the window.

"Don't accuse me. It's not me!" expostulated Ginger. "I have seen the light. I am no longer living in darkness. I am born again!"

Epilogue

One late afternoon, Miss Grant received a luxury envelope. Inside it was enclosed an invitation card. How Emily Grant received it remained a mystery! With Joy, Emily's face lit up. She expected the invitation. Mr Burrows mentioned it to her as he engaged in conversation. He interrupted the guests who were speaking. Meeting Mr Burrows at a get-together.

Emily was unsurprised by his invitation to a ball. Mr Burrows' warm invitation to the ball was personal.

Emily put an invitation card against an oriental vase on the mantlepiece. She felt happy about his personal invitation. She was pleased. She looked forward to the summer ball. Everything else seemed unsurprisingly uninteresting. With boredom with regard to anything else, she lost complete interest once again.

Miss Grant fantasised about the ball, dreaming of it. She romanticised. She was overjoyed at her fantasies. She engaged in her dreams, her delirious, exciting ecstasies, a thrill of pleasure.

Miss Grant took off her hat. She fanned herself. She stood and looked at herself in the wall mirror in admiring narcissism.

- THE END -

*Available worldwide from
Amazon and all good bookstores*

www.mtp.agency

www.facebook.com/mtp.agency

@mtp_agency

www.ingramcontent.com/pod-product-compliance
Lightning Source LLC
LaVergne TN
LVHW011739060526
838200LV00051B/3244